Richard Lovell Edgeworth, James C. Charlemont

A Letter to the Right Hon. the Earl of Charlemont

on the tellograph and on the defence of Ireland

Richard Lovell Edgeworth, James C. Charlemont

A Letter to the Right Hon. the Earl of Charlemont
on the tellograph and on the defence of Ireland

ISBN/EAN: 9783337381936

Printed in Europe, USA, Canada, Australia, Japan

Cover: Foto ©Andreas Hilbeck / pixelio.de

More available books at **www.hansebooks.com**

A

LETTER

TO THE

RIGHT HON, THE EARL OF CHARLEMONT

ON THE

TELLOGRAPH,

AND ON THE

DEFENCE OF IRELAND.

———

By RICHARD LOVELL EDGEWORTH, Esq.

F. R. S. AND M. R. I. A.

———

To take the management of any affair of public concern from the man, who has almoft brought it to a conclufion, is regarded as the moft invidious injuftice.

ADAM SMITH.

———

DUBLIN: PRINTED.

LONDON, RE-PRINTED FOR J. JOHNSON, IN ST. PAUL'S CHURCH YARD.

———

1797.

[Price ONE SHILLING.]

LETTER

TO THE

EARL OF CHARLEMONT, &c.

———

MY LORD,

Sʜᴏʀᴛʟʏ after I had the honour of feeing you in England, in 1792, I heard that difturbances had broken out in Ireland.—The revolution in France, and the political fituation of Ireland had a connection, which could not efcape the eye of the moft fuperficial obferver. I therefore refolved to return, and to contribute, whatever talents and acquirements I poffeffed to the common caufe. I built and improved, I employed numerous tradefmen and labourers, as if the country were in perfect fecurity; and in the dreadful fcenes which afterwards occurred, I have the fatisfaction to fay no tenant on my eftate was ever convicted or ever accufed — nor has a defender been found, even amongft my workmen. As a grand juror, a magiftrate, and a country gentleman, I endeavoured to perform my duty, and to abide fteadily between the extremes of vio-

lence

lence and inaction. When I heard of the French Telegraph a new object arose for my exertions. I recalled to my mind experiments that I had tried so long ago as the year 1767, when I had practised this species of aerial communication; and thinking that it might be peculiarly useful to this country, I constructed some machines with which I conversed, in August 1794, between Packenham Hall, (the seat of Lord Longford,) and Edgeworthstown. Finding my success equal to my expectations, I was advised by the present Bishop of Offory, who expected the arrival of Lord Fitzwilliam, to shew my invention to some gentleman, whose opinion would be attended to by administration.—I naturally recurred to the Speaker, with whom I had been bred up, and with whose friendship I had been always honoured; he immediately understood and approved the contrivance, gave me the warmest encouragement, and during the months of September, October, and November, he assisted me in trying experiments, and in constructing the plan of a vocabulary; a work of no small difficulty and labour.

In February, 1795, the Bishop of Offory at my request presented a memorial to Lord Fitzwilliam, which I am informed was approved of, and which would in all probability have been attended to, if Lord Fitzwilliam had remained in Ireland.

The Speaker had advised me to prepare a chain

of

of Tellographs * from his houfe to Dublin, and in
confequence I had erected machines at Collon, Bellewftown, Ratoath, and Mulhuddar, and under his
aufpices, in fpring 1795, I prefented the following
memorial to Lord Camden.

No.

* In November and December, 1794, the following para-
graphs, written by fome perfon unknown to me, appeared in the
Irifh and Englifh newfpapers.

Drogheda, November 19th.

The Right Hon. the Speaker of the Houfe of Commons, has
been the firft in this country to prove the expediency of ufing
the Telegraph; on Saturday lâft one was erected on Mount
Oriel, near the fpeaker's at Collon, and another on the hill of
Skreene, in the county of Meath, fifteen miles diftant, where
each party took their ftation, and when the neceffary fignals
were made, they communicated to, and anfwered each other at
that diftance, in the fpace of five minutes.

The whole apparatus is nothing more than a triangular ftand
of about 14 feet in height, placed on an eminence, at the top of
which is fixed an index, which turns on a fwivel: the index has
eight different fituations in the circle it defcribes, fignifying the
eight figures, viz. 0, 1, 2, 3, 4, 5, 6, and 7. The perfon at the
correfponding ftation, taken fuppofe fifteen miles off, can clearly
perceive by the help of a good telefcope, every fituation of the
index, and each party at each fituation is furnifhed with a glof-
fary or dictionary, to explain the fignals, and thus the ideas of
the one, may in a few minutes be communicated to the other.

In the Star, October 10, 1796, the following defcription of
the *new* French Telegraph appeared. It is obvious that it is
conftructed upon the very fame principles as mine, defcribed in
the paragraph, which I have juft quoted.

" THE TELEGRAPH.—A new machine of this defcription
" has been lately erected on the top of the Pavilion of Unity,
A 3   " which

No. I.

A PROPOSAL,

Addreſſed to His Excellency the Lord Lieutenant of Ireland,

For the eſtabliſhment of a corps of men, to convey
ſecret and ſwift intelligence.

In the preſent ſtate of Europe, and of Ireland in
particular, it is unneceſſary to expatiate upon the

" which forms a part of the palace of the Thuilleries, and
" which is to communicate with Germany, by a correſponding
" chain extending as far as Landau.

" In the erection of this machine, which differs materially
" from that of Chappe, every attention has been paid to its
" improvement.—It now conſiſts of a large beam, painted
" black, and fixed horizontally on four large poſts ; attached
" to the main beam are five diſtinct arms, ſimilar to the ſecon-
" dary arms of the other Telegraph.—There are two other
" arms attached to the two central poſts, the former five have
" each eight poſitions, two vertical, four inclined, and two ho-
" rizontal, &c. &c.

" The number of changes, though apparently beyond the
" circumſtances of the caſe, will enable the conductors of the
" machine to ſubſtitute words for letters, and thus not only to
" accelerate this communication but to make it uſeful, not only
" to the purpoſes of government, but to thoſe of individuals on
" particular occaſions."

The idea of my Tellograph, is to point out diviſions by a
hand or index on an imaginary circle—no change in the form
can conceal this principle. *Tellograph* is the name I give to my
machine, to denote, that it conveys words inſtead of letters.—
An engraving and deſcription of it will ſoon appear in the
Tranſactions of the R. I. Academy.

utility

utility of fpeedy, and fecret intelligence; it is fufficient to fay, that if the eye of government can be
enabled to fee the whole country like a Map before
it, and if its orders can be conveyed by day or
night, in a few minutes to every part of the kingdom, its energy muft be increafed beyond the limits
of ordinary fpeculation; and if fuch a mode of communication be extended to Great Britain, another
incalculable fource of advantage would be opened
to both kingdoms.——If inftant notice can be given
of alarm upon the coafts, or of domeftic difturbance,
the force of government can be directed to the
point of danger; unfounded rumours can be ftopped
in their progrefs, and incipient combinations can be
broken, before they increafe to any formidable
magnitude; inferior depredations would become
lefs frequent, as offenders could fcarcely efcape from
punifhment—almoft as foon as an offence was com-
mitted it would be known at every bridge and
outlet of the diftrict where it happened; a defcription of the offender would meet him wherever
he went, and a force would every where be ready
to arreft him.

If with great celerity of communication entire
fecrecy can be connected; if it be impoffible that
any perfon concerned in the bufinefs, can decypher
the intelligence which he is employed to convey;
if the mode of communication can be indefinitely
varied without difficulty or confufion; if the advantages of fuch an eftablifhment extend to peace as

well

well as war, in preferving domeftic fecurity, in promoting the exchange of commodities, in facilitating the bufinefs of infurance, in preventing frauds in lotteries, in equalizing the prices of grain, and of other merchandize ; and, in fhort, if they may be felt in every intercourfe of fociety, there can remain but one objeƈt to be confidered—the expence of the eftablifhment : this muft vary with the extent of the correfpondence.

Perhaps thirty permanent ftations would be fufficient for the whole kingdom.—In hazy weather, portable machines may be detached from thefe ftations to keep up the communication. Where it is neceffary that the permanent ftations fhould be tenable againft mufketry or fudden violence, each ftation would coft about three hundred pounds ; where temporary eftablifhments fhould be thought fufficient, half the expence might be faved.

The men who are employed fhould be under military difcipline, to fecure their punƈtuality and obedience ; but as they can be employed in the place of other foldiers, in affiftance of the civil power, their expence fhould not be charged exclufively to this eftablifhment.

To conduƈt this bufinefs, Mr. Edgeworth propofes to raife a corps of men, under any denomination that may be thought proper, and to have them inftruƈted, not only in the praƈtice of conveying intelligence,

telligence, but in the art of throwing up field works, and in the management of light arms.

Mr. Edgeworth has, at no fmall expence, both of time and money, brought his plan to fuch perfection, that he is willing to eftablifh a correfpondence between any places his Excellency fhall point out, and to fuffer the whole lofs, if his plan fhall be found deficient either in fecrecy or expedition.

RICHARD LOVELL EDGEWORTH,
F. R. S. AND M R. I. A.

September 14*th*, 1794.

Prefented to Lord CAMDEN, May 3.th, 1795.

After his Excellency had glanced his eye over the title of my memorial, he was pleafed to fay, that fuch an eftablifhment did not appear to him neceffary, but that he would confult my friend, the Speaker; from whom I afterwards heard, that my plan would not be purfued. Laft September, when the alarm of an invafion refounded in every part of the kingdom, as foon as I heard that preparations were actually making againft fuch an event, I wrote the following letter to Lord Carhampton; who had feen the Tellograph at Edgeworthftown, and had expreffed his approbation of its performance.

No. II.

MY LORD,

IT is rumoured that an invafion of this country is thought poffible, and that means of defence are

under

under confideration.—I beg leave to requeft that your lordfhip will offer my fervices, to convey intelligence from the coaft * to government, at my own expence.

It is my duty, or perhaps my whim, to wifh that my fmall fkill as an engineer fhould be really ufeful; and I apply to your lordfhip in particular to make this offer in my name, becaufe when I had the honour of feeing you, you appeared to think that the country required protection.

I have the honour to be my lord, &c.

RICHARD LOVELL EDGEWORTH.

September 8th, 1796.

No. III.

Lord CARHAMPTON's anfwer to my letter was as follows.

DEAR SIR, *Dublin, September 6th.*

IF you will be good enough to come up to town, my Lord Lieutenant will be glad to converfe with you on the fubject of the Tellograph, and I truft you will be employed.

I am, dear Sir,

with great truth,

your faithful fervant,

CARHAMPTON.

* The coaft of Wicklow was at that time fuppofed to be the moft in danger.

On

On the twelfth, I waited on the Lord Lieutenant, who converfed with me fome time upon the fubject; his Excellency afked me what would be the expence of a communication between Dublin and Cork, and in what time it could be completed ?— I anfwered—that with the affiftance of machinery, which I had ready, and which was at the fervice of government, a *temporary* eftablifhment might be formed in a month, and kept up for a year, at the expence of £.700.—His Excellency defired to know whether fuch an eftablifhment could not be formed in lefs than a month?—I replied, that a prudent man would not promife it.—His Excellency then defired me to prepare for an experiment before him; the time for which, he faid, fhould be fhortly appointed.—His Excellency informed me that Mr. Pelham had engaged a perfon belonging to the Admiralty Telegraph, to come over to eftablifh it here, and he was fo good as to add, that he was forry my propofal in 1795 had not been accepted.

I returned my acknowledgments to his Excellency, but with refpect to entering into any competition with the Admiralty Telegraph, I affured him, that fuch had never been my intention; I had no defign to interfere with any other perfon's intereft or invention, my propofal related folely to this country, and my wifh was purely *to make myfelf ufeful in the manner beft fuited to my fituation and capacity.*

After this converfation, I returned to the coun-

try,

try, and with the utmoft expedition completed feven new Tellographs, of an improved conftruction.— Thofe, which I had firft employed, were intended for fixed ftations, and therefore were more cumberfome, and required ftands of great folidity.—My new machines were contrived to fhut up like umbrellas, and were furnifhed with portable ftands.— They were of different fizes: 6, 10, 11, 12, 20 feet; to fhew by experiments at different diftances, that a Tellograph could be *read off* with a telefcope, upon any fpot which could be barely feen with the naked eye.

No. IV.

I wrote the following letter to Mr. PELHAM.

SIR, *Edgeworthftown, September 19th, 1796.*
In obedience to Lord Camden's commands, I have prepared Tellographs, with which I am ready to try an experiment before his Excellency, whenever he thinks proper; I have alfo collected fome machines, which I ufed in my firft trials, and which I could employ immediately, to form a temporary communication between Cork and Dublin.

I fuppofe, that with a corps of four hundred men, and with an expence of four or five thoufand pounds, a communication might be eftablifhed between Dublin and the following places, Brayhead, Wicklow, Wexford, Waterford, Dungarvan, Youghal, Cork,

Cork, Limerick, Galway, Sligo, Loughfoyle, Belfaſt, and Carlingford, beſides an extenſive inland correſpondence; part of this corps might be employed in keeping up a ſpeedy intercourſe between the troops of a cordon with my portable Tellograph, which a man can carry, and can ſet up in five minutes, and which is legible in weather when other Telegraphs are ineffectual.

I have the honour to be, with great reſpect,
Sir,
Your moſt obedient ſervant,
RICHARD LOVELL EDGEWORTH.

No. V.

To this Letter Mr. PELHAM replied.

SIR, *Phœnix Park, September 26th,* 1796.
I HAVE received the honour of your letter, ſtating, that you have prepared ſome Tellographs in obedience to the Lord Lieutenant's commands, and that you were ready to make an experiment before his Excellency. I am to inform you, that his Excellency will be very glad to ſee the experiment at any time that may be moſt convenient to you; and I ſhall be obliged to you if you will give me a day's notice. The end of this week would be an eligible time if it ſuited you.

I am, Sir,
Your moſt obedient ſervant,
T. PELHAM.

I imme-

I immediately went up to town, and I was defired to wait on Mr. Pelham, at his houfe in the Park, on the 2d of October.—The Secretary at war and the Secretary for the civil department were at breakfaft with him. He afked to fee the portable reconnoitring Tellograph, which I had brought with me, and a fpecimen of my vocabulary. Though I had no perfon with me who underftood the management of the machines but my fervant, Mr. Pelham defired to fee them tried. Mr. Cooke and Mr. Elliot, the two fecretaries, whom I did not know, obligingly offered to affift me. They took one of the Tellographs to the * butts in the Park, and Mr. Pelham received a meffage from them in the lawn before his houfe.

Mr. Pelham, and the gentlemen who were with him, exprefied much fatisfaction at the experiment, and he informed me that the Lord Lieutenant was to go the next day to Collon, and afked me if I could meet him there.

My machines were at this time on their road to

* When the two Secretaries had taken poffeffion of the butts for their experiment, they were arrefted by a centinel, who confidered them as perfons that muft have fome evil defign in view, from the ftrange apparatus they had with them.—It was in vain that the Secretary at war declared who he was, the centinel would not liberate him till he was convinced of his identity.

The laughter which this occafioned, and the good humour with which thefe gentlemen behaved, made me form agreeable hopes as to my future tranfactions with them.

Dublin, I difpatched a fervant to take them acrofs the country by night, to Collon; two of my fons carried machines to Bellewftown, eleven Irifh miles diftance from Collon.

Notwithftanding the coldnefs of the weather, and a brifk ftorm, the next morning Lord Camden had the complaifance to remain two hours on a bleak hill to fee the experiment. It fucceeded to my wifhes, and his Excellency was pleafed to fay, that he was entirely fatisfied. He further affured me *that no other Telegraph fhould be employed in this country in preference to mine.*

At Mr. Pelham's defire, I fent a written propo-fal for a Tellographic communication, of which the following is a copy.

No. VI.

MEMORIAL,

PRESENTED OCTOBER 6TH, 1796.

Mr. Edgeworth will undertake to convey intelli-gence from Dublin to Cork, and back to Dublin, by means of fourteen or fifteen different ftations, at the rate of one hundred pounds per annum, for each ftation, as long as government fhall think proper; and from Dublin to any other place at the fame rate, in proportion to the diftance.—Pro-vided,

vided, that when government choofes to difcontinue
the bufinefs, they fhall pay one year's contract,
over and above the current expence, as fome com-
penfation for the prime coft of the apparatus, and
the trouble of the firft eftablifhment.

This memorial was accompanied with the following
letter to Mr. PELHAM.

No. VII.

SIR,   *Collon, October* 1796.

I ENCLOSE a propofal for eftablifhing a Tellograph
between Dublin and Cork, &c. that fomething fpe-
cific may be immediately before you.

I was advifed not to diftract attention by more
propofals than one, and it was fuggefted, that if a
Tellographic corps were eftablifhed, the men at
each ftation would be under the command of any
officer who might be in the neighbourhood, which
would interrupt my proceedings, and would put
my conduct, and refponfibility, into the hands of
other perfons.—This might furely be obviated by
general orders from the Commander in chief—I
cannot therefore help thinking, that it would be
beft to eftablifh a corps of men in ftations, tenable
againft a mob and againft mufketry.—That one
company fhould be employed for attending the

army

army, for reconnoitring, &c. &c. That this company fhould be changed from time to time, to re-
lieve the centinels on watch.

The whole eftablifhments, independently of the
corps, would, if the ftations were only common
houfes, coft about four or five thoufand pounds.——
If they were made tenable, the expence would be
about fix or feven thoufand pounds, to convey intelligence to every part of the kingdom which
fhould be neceffary. — If a civil eftablifhment is
adopted, it appears to me, that the men, who muft
protect it, would be an additional expence—on a
military plan, the men who protect, might conduct
it.

For my own part, I am fenfible that you com-
prehend the whole of the bufinefs—that you fee the
great difference that there muft be between a partial
and a general plan, *and I am perfectly willing to purfue, without referve, any plan that you fhall approve.*

I beg leave to offer my acknowledgments for the
goodnefs of his Excellency, and for your liberality
and kindnefs.

I have the honour to be, &c.

RICHARD LOVELL EDGEWORTH.

During the converfation that paffed at Collon,
Mr. Pelham told me, that the Duke of York had
expreffed a wifh for a reconnoitring Telegraph,
and that he thought mine was exactly what his

B   Royal

Royal Highnefs wanted.—By the 10th I had a new portable Tellograph, conftructed in the handfomeft manner in my power; it contained a telefcope in its axletree, fo as to be manageable by a fingle perfon. Mr. Pelham examined this at his houfe in the Park, and did me the honour to accept of it as a prefent.—He afked me, if I had any friend to whom it would be an object to prefent it in his name to the Duke of York. — I mentioned Mr. Bridgeman Edgeworth my ward, who belongs to the Woolwich Academy.—Mr. Pelham lamented, that fending for Mr. Bridgeman Edgeworth from England, to inftruct him in the management of the machine, would wafte much time.—My fon Lovell, who was prefent at this converfation, offered to go over to England, to teach his relation what might perhaps be of advantage to him.—Mr. Pelham immediately propofed, that government fhould defray Mr. Lovell Edgeworth's expences—this my fon in the moft proper manner declined, by faying, " that even his father fhould not defray his expences upon fuch an occafion."—He was thanked, and applauded, and as foon as with the utmoft induftry another Tellograph was completed, he was difpatched to London with a letter from Mr. Pelham to the Duke of York, a letter to Colonel Brownrigg his Royal Highnefs's Secretary, and with other letters of recommendation. In the whole of this bufinefs, I was much captivated with Mr. Pelham's politenefs, and I had fufficient opportunity of feeing the clearnefs and extent of his underftanding. Upon a fubject entirely

new

new to him, he became immediately acquainted with the whole detail of my machinery—with the conftruction of the vocabulary—with the difference, which fhould be obferved between a vocabulary for common ufe, and one which might be conftructed for an univerfal language—and with all the important purpofes to which fuch an invention could be applied.—He informed me that he had written to Lord Grenville, to recommend an eftablifhment of the Tellograph between England and Ireland, and added, " *That if the* Englifh miniftry did not concur in fuch and eftablifhment, *it was ftill in the power of government here, to do what they thought proper.*"

On the 28th of October, Mr. Bridgeman Edgeworth and my fon obtained an audience of the Duke of York; and on the next day they fhewed the portable reconnoitring Tellograph in Kenfington gardens to his Royal Highnefs, who expreffed his approbation in a moft gracious manner. Colonel Brownrigg, the Duke of York's Secretary, engaged my fon to meet him the next day at the Admiralty, that he and the Duke's Aid-de-camp might learn the management of the machine, and the ufe of the vocabulary.—Sir William Fawcett was prefent; he feemed much pleafed, and gave it as his opinion, that the reconnoitring Tellograph might be employed in the Weft Indies to great advantage.

Before my fon left London, Colonel Brownrigg prefented him, from the Duke of York, with a

B 2   handfome

handfome refracting telefcope, upon which he was permitted to infcribe his Royal Highnefs's name.

During this time I had no doubt, that arrangements were making for an eftablifhment of my Tellograph in Ireland, the idea of extending it to Scotland to meet the Englifh Telegraph had been taken up by Mr. Pelham; but as to this country, I had never fuppofed that any thing was in fufpenfe, except the mode of the eftablifhment, whether it fhould be civil or military? —As foon as an adjournment of parliament took place, I went to town and waited upon Mr. Pelham —he was much hurried with bufinefs, but from the moment I faw him, I could perceive that the views of government had changed, and after a few words of converfation he promifed to write to me, and the following is a copy of his letter.

No. VIII.

Dublin Caftle, November 17th, 1796.

DEAR SIR,

THE Lord Lieutenant communicated to Lord Spencer your plan for eftablifhing a communication of intelligence between Cork and Dublin, and between Dublin and Belfaft and Donaghadee, by means of a Tellograph of your invention, and requefted to know whether fuch an eftablifhment would be of fuch advantage to Great Britain, as to induce Lord Spencer to encourage the adoption of it.

Lord

Lord Spencer and the Board of Admiralty did not think it would be of fuch importance, as to induce them to encourage his Excellency in making the experiment. His Excellency thinking the invention a very ingenious one, and wifhing to fhew every degree of attention to you in the bufinefs, confulted the Commander in Chief upon the advantages to be derived from fuch an eftablifhment for the communication of intelligence within the kingdom; and not receiving more encouragement from him, than he had done from the Admiralty in England, his Excellency has directed me to fay, that much as he admires the invention, and the motives which engaged the author to apply his talents to this object, he does not fee any purpofe in this country, for which he could be warranted in incurring the expence.

The utility of a Tellograph may hereafter be confidered greater; but I truft that at all events, thofe talents which have been directed to this 'purfuit will be turned to fome other object, and that the public will have the benefit of that extraordinary activity and zeal, which I have witneffed on this occafion, in . fome other inftitution, which I am fure that the ingenuity of the author will not require much time to fuggeft.

I have the honour to be, with great refpect,

dear Sir,

Your moft obedient humble fervant,

T. PELHAM.

 No.

No. IX.

Mr. EDGEWORTH's anſwer.

Edgeworthſtown, November 21ſt, 1796.

SIR,

WHEN I had the honor of ſeeing you, I ſtated, that my Lord Carhampton's ·opinion was, *that I ſhould be employed*; which will appear by the en-cloſed copy of his Lordſhips letter of the 6th of September *.

What new circumſtances have occurred to leſſen alarm, or make my ſervices unacceptable, I am at a loſs to conjecture. My invention however has been adopted at the Admiralty, by the Duke of York's Chaplain, with ſuch ſlight alteration as can-not blind the public, to whoſe judgment I ſhall ſoon ſubmit the whole tranſaction.

I am, Sir,

Your moſt obedient humble ſervant,

RICHARD LOVELL EDGEWORTH.

I have, my Lord, in a ſhort and plain narrative, laid before your Lordſhip and the public, the whole of what has paſſed between government and me re-lative to the Tellograph; and I ſhall now beg leave to make a few remarks upon the ſubject.

In 1795, when my propoſal † was preſented to

* No. III.   † No. I

Lord

Lord Camden, the anfwer which I received gave me *no encouragement* ; his Excellency faw no neceffity at that time for fuch an eftablifhment : this was a dif-tinct anfwer, of which I had no reafon to complain ; but in September, 1796, when Mr. Pelham had engaged a perfon from England, to bring over the Admiralty Telegraph to this country, when that perfon had actually arrived, it was plain that go-vernment had changed their opinion with regard to the utility of fuch an eftablifhment, and when I was fent for by Lord Camden, and defired by his Ex-cellency to prepare Tellographs for an experiment before him, when he had inquired from me an efti-mate of the expence of a temporary eftablifhment for immediate ufe, and had particularly been earneft with refpect to the time within which it could be completed, had I not reafon to fuppofe, that nothing but a proof of the practicability of my propofal was wanting ? When a nobleman of high honour and fuperior abilities had written to me " that he trufted, I fhould be employed *," when Mr. Pelham † had defired me to bring up to town the machines which I had prepared, fome of which were exprefsly men-tioned ‡ as being intended for a communication from Dublin to Cork, when the fimplicity of the ma-chinery, and the impenetrable fecrecy of the mode of communication were applauded by every mem-ber of adminiftration, who had feen them—and when my invention was finally approved of by the

* No. II.   † No. IV.   ‡ No. V.

Lord

Lord Lieutenant himfelf, who gave it in the handfomeft manner a decided preference to any that he
had heard of, was I too fanguine in concluding,
that the general queſtion of expediency had been
previoufly confidered ?—Did it appear in any degree probable, that gentlemen ſhould take and give
fo much trouble about a thing which they did not
mean to purfue ?—Had the incompetency of the
invention, or the *extravagance* of its expence, been
the reafons affigned for the rejection of my propofal, and had it appeared that a better or a cheaper
mode of communication than mine had been at the
command of adminiſtration, their conduct would have
been in fome degree juſtifiable.—But the contrivance was approved of; and the expence was not
one fourth of what the government in England paid
for the Admiralty Telegraph. That the expence
could not have been the real objection, is evident
from this fingle circumſtance — Mr. Pelham had
been informed of the expence of the Admiralty Telegraph, and had notwithſtanding brought over a
perfon from the Admiralty, on purpofe to eſtabliſh
a communication between Cork and Dublin.

The expence of the Engliſh Telegraph between
Portfmouth and London, a diſtance of fifty-fix
Iriſh miles, is three thoufand pounds a year.—My
offer for an eſtabliſhment between Dublin and Cork,
a diſtance of one hundred and twenty Iriſh miles,
was upon an eſtimate of one thoufand four hundred
pounds per annum. At the rate of the Engliſh
Telegraph

Telegraph it would have coft fix thoufand fix hundred pounds—a fum for which, with a very fmall
addition, I would have eftablifhed Tellographs at
every important ftation upon the coaft.

I do not mean to affert that government ever
made me a *pofitive promife*, but if any doubt can remain whether government gave me encouragement
to proceed, let us reflect upon the character and
conduct of Mr. Pelham.—Would he have fuffered
my reconnoitring Tellograph to be taken to England, where, as it refembled in miniature my other
machines, it would fubject them to imitation * ; or
would he have permitted Mr. Lovell Edgeworth to
have gone to London, on purpofe to have it prefented to the Duke of York, if he had not intended
that my plan fhould be adopted in this kingdom?
Mr. Pelham in his letter to Colonel Brownrigg exprefsly mentioned, that my fon went for no other
purpofe to England; and to me he expreffed in
diftinct terms, that if the Englifh adminiftration
fhould not concur in the fcheme of communicating
intelligence from London to Dublin, " it would
" ftill be in the power of government here, to do

---

* By the fame poft which brought Mr. Pelham's letter
(page 20) I received a letter from London, which informed
me, that a Tellograph upon the fame principle as mine was juft
fet up at the Admiralty by the Duke of York's Chaplain.
Since thefe fheets went to the prefs I have learned, that the
machine which was then erected, had been contrived fome
weeks before mine had been taken to England.

4   " what

" what they pleafed in the bufinefs."—I could
fcarcely after what had paffed fuppofe, that what
they pleafed was *nothing*.—For it muft be obferved,
that no attempt was made to accommodate the
bufinefs in any manner to my feelings. I had offered to eftablifh a communication from the coaft to
Dublin at my own expence *,—of this offer no notice was taken: I had already, as was known to
government, expended £500: as much more
would have erected a *temporary* eftablifhment (for
perhaps a year) to Cork; and by this trifling complaifance, the utility of my invention might have
been fairly tried, and the moft prudential government upon earth, could not accufe itfelf of extravagance in being partner with a private gentleman
in an experiment, which had with inferior apparatus, and at four times the expence, been tried and
approved of in France and England.

I muft alfo remark, that I had carefully avoided
all competition with the Admiralty Telegraph; my
propofals were confined to Ireland †, and the idea
of meeting the Englifh Telegraph at Portpatrick
was a fecondary confideration, which might, if a
national eftablifhment took place within this kingdom, be adopted at a fortnight's notice.

The attempt to throw the rejection of my propofal upon the Commander in Chief, is beft an-

* No. I.   † No. VII.

fwered

fwered by his own letter; in which he tells me,
" that on the day upon which he fent for me by
" the Lord Lieutenant's command, he had found
" his Excellency and Admiral Kingfmill confulting
" on the expediency of fending for a Telegraph
" from England; that he warmly recommended
" my being employed in preference to any other
" perfon, but that *the taking up originally the idea*
" *of Telegraphs, and giving it up, were both unknown*
" *to him.*"

As to Mr. Pelham, I think he has been obliged
to act againft his feelings; for befides the politenefs of his conduct to me, his letter * is flatter-
ing in the extreme—fome parts of it might from
another perfon be confidered as ironical; but I
firmly believe, that it was written with kindnefs.—
He defires me to turn my talents to fome other
fcheme for the public good, thinking (I fincerely
hope) that my views are directed to that honeft
purpofe.—But he forgot, that all my former ef-
forts had been rendered ineffectual by caufes
which I could not counteract, and that in any new
purfuit for the benefit of the public, I could expect nothing but unavailing labour, fruitlefs expence,
and irretrievable lofs of time.—Fortune has enabled me to bear the lofs of a confiderable fum,
without inconvenience; but had I been poor, I
fhould not have met with more confideration.

* No. VIII.

Figure

Figure to yourfelf, my Lord—for you can feel for your inferiors—the defpair of an ingenious, friendlefs man, who had beftowed the bread of his family in perfecting a projeft, which ought to have been adopted for its utility; figure to yourfelf fuch a man, lured on beyond the bounds of prudence, by the fallacious hopes of remuneration, receiving at laft a cold negative, and difmiffed to wretchednefs and a prifon.—If this publication can fave one fuch man from ruin, my expence, and time, and labour, have been well beftowed.

Some years ago, a Minifter in England (the ftory would fuit many of his fucceffors) fent for an ingenious man, to whofe talents he had been indebted, and advifed him to learn Spanifh. — After three months labour, the pale ftudent prefented himfelf, and modeftly hinted, that he had made a confiderable progrefs in that language; but inftead of being appointed fecretary to a Spanifh embaffy, or conful to fome Spanifh port, he was *politely* told, " that " he was prepared to tafte the fublime pleafure of " reading *Don Quixote* in the original."

I am not fo utterly unacquainted with courts, as not to be aware, that I have neglefted fome of thofe arts which are fuppofed (I hope unjuftly) to be effential to fuccefs;—I was early advifed by an experienced friend, to leave the cutting and carving of the bufinefs to government; if I had connefted this advice with what I have heard upon other

other occafions, and inftead of labouring to fhow economy and difintereftednefs, had I introduced my Tellograph in the form of a lucrative job, in which there might be good picking for others, I might have increafed the number of my *friends*, and have gratified thofe who are in power, by an opportunity of increafing patronage.—To him, who is not in Parliament, every ftep in public bufinefs is arduous.—When Lewis XIV. afked a lady, "how he could find the way to her chamber?"— fhe anfwered —" Par l'Eglife." — The fhorteft way perhaps to the Caftle, is through the Houfe of Commons.—Independently of all interefted or am- bitious motives, there feems to be fome ftrange delight in political corruption. There are men who imagine that there is fomething humourous, ingenu- ous, liberal, and graceful, in the frank avowal of venality.

I once applied to a gentleman (who had niched himfelf comfortably in a feat at a lucrative Board) for his affiftance upon a certain bufinefs then before Parliament—" Tell me honeftly, my good friend," faid he, " is it a job ?—If it is, I will attend—if it is not, the thing muft make its way by its *merits*."

Many will perhaps be furprifed, that after my opportunities of learning *better*, I fhould not have availed myfelf of my knowledge of the world— To thefe I can only reply in the language of a per-
fecuted

fecuted Statefman, who, among corrupt Courtiers, had the misfortune to preferve his integrity,

"Il feroit aifé de vous imiter, mais il éft difficile de s'y refoudre."

I am impatient, my Lord, to finifh this part of my fubject, that I may lay afide the conftant repetition of " the moft difgufting of all the pronouns *," which has hitherto been the unfuccefsful hero of my tale.—But he who puts his name to what he writes, refpects the liberty of the prefs, and fets an example, which, if it were followed, would difcountenance the effufions of anonymous malice and fcurrility.

Whoever appeals to the public, encounters a dangerous dilemma ;—if he expect the fympathy of mankind, he muft not only convince them that he is injured, but that he feels the injury ; for it is a contradiction in terms to talk of fympathizing with him who does not *feel*. On the contrary, if a man fhews quick fenfibility, the warmth of his refentment alarms the caution of his readers ; it is fuppofed that objects are magnified through the mift of paffion, and it is believed that a man with the beft intentions in the world is not to be trufted, and fhould not truft himfelf, whilft he is under the influence of any violent emotion. To avoid thefe extremes is not difficult to him who is really interefted for the

* Gibbon's Life.

publc,

public, who is perfectly happy in his private life, and who is difappointed more in what concerns others than in what touches himfelf. Mankind will juftly fhare the indignation which he feels for the defertion of their intereft, and will go beyond his refentment for any neglect with which one who wifhed to have been their benefactor has been treated. My motto expreffes what I think the public will feel on my account.

I fhall now endeavour to fhew, that the object which I purfued was national, and that the nation has a right to inquire why it was laid afide.

When I fpeak of Tellographs as ferious means of protection, I muft explain myfelf, and I hope I may be pardoned if I fhould repeat any ideas I have already fuggefted in my memorials, becaufe I have obferved, that memorials as well as prefaces are feldom read.

In this country, objects of fcience have not been much attended to, but the genius of the nation is now awake; and the neceffity of employing every refource of art muft foon be acknowledged.—Suppofe that two or three different fquadrons menaced the coafts of Ireland, or perhaps the coafts of both countries, what muft be the firft wifh of an intelligent General?—Surely to know as foon as poffible the real object of the enemy.—It is commonly fuppofed, that the South-eaft coaft of the kingdom

would

would be the object of invasion; the West and Northern coasts appear to me to be the most in danger. I had formed this opinion long before I saw the same idea expressed in an excellent pamphlet " *On the Defence of Ireland*," which has been withheld, I do not know for what reason, from the public. Whatever difference of opinion there may be, as to the parts of our coast which require most to be guarded, the enemy would, at all events, endeavour to effect a landing where it was the least expected, and would by every possible means distract our attention.—Our having the certainty of intelligence, must either oblige them to concentrate their force, or would baffle any attempt to divide ours.—It has been suggested, and believed, that foreign enemies have artfully endeavoured to foment insurrections amongst the people of Ireland.—Had any such plan been concerted to distract the country by exciting disturbances amongst the populace, would not a speedy communication of intelligence between every part of the kingdom and government, be one of the most useful means of counteracting such designs?—Apprized of the real circumstances and extent of the danger, ministers would be able to regulate their conduct accordingly; proper assistance might be afforded to the civil power, and the provincial forces might rapidly be collected at the necessary point.

Are these objects of no consequence? Does the security of Ireland depend merely upon the physical

sical force, which can be collected in its defence ?
And what part of the physical force of Ireland can
be relied upon for its defence ?—one half?—one
third ?—one tenth of its male inhabitants ?—Surely
if force is to be relied upon, that force muft require
skill to direct, and ingenuity to increafe it, nor
should any refource of human invention be neg-
lected, which promifes even problematical or remote advantages !—Is the government of Ireland
afraid, that too many applications of this fort should
be made by Gentlemen ?—Is the attention of the
kingdom too much turned to fcience ?—Perhaps
the ferpent by which the ancients perfonified invention, is one of that fpecies which will not live upon
Irifh ground.—To object to the expence of fix or
feven thoufand pounds, and the employment of
three or four hundred men, upon an object of national importance, is to raife the value of money
higher, and to fink the value of protection lower
than has been yet attempted by any Statefman, *who
was liable to refponfibility.*

Of late it has been the policy of government to
affect alarm ; it was during one of thefe fits either
of real or pretended apprehenfion, that Minifters
expreffed fuch an earneft defire to have a Tellograph eftablifhed in this kingdom.—A month appeared to the Lord Lieutenant too long a time to
allow for the completion of fuch an eftablifhment
between Dublin and Cork !—A month paffed away,
the danger continued the fame, but the means of

C   defence,

defe nce, which had been fo anxioufly fought, became " *unneceffary.*"

The moft favourable fuppofition, by which we
can account for the conduct of the Irifh government in this bufinefs is, that a fuperior influence in
England forbade our adminiftration to proceed.—
If this be the fact, I can only deplore their humi-
liating ftate of tutelage.

It muft be mortifying to a Viceroy, who comes
over to Ireland with enlarged views, and benevo-
lent intentions, to difcover, when he attempts to
act for himfelf, that he is peremptorily checked by
foreign influence; that a circle is chalked round
him, beyond which he cannot, or he fancies that
he cannot.move.

It is in vain that we attempt to ftudy the .cha-
racter of our Governors, if in fact their difpofitions
have no influence on their conduct.—In the fuccef-
fion of Vice-Royalty in Ireland, there is an automa-
tic uniformity; there is no change but in the form,
that holds the delegated fceptre; — perhaps this
change is fufficient to amufe the credulous populace,
but fuch of the fpectators, as are curious to know
the machinery of the fpectacle, muft look for the
hand that holds the wires, and liften to the voice
that fpeaks behind the fcenes.

It is not impoffible, that the Englifh government

4

may

may have been glad to take advantage of an alarm of invasion in this kingdom, to induce the gentlemen of Ireland to arm themselves at * their own expence in its defence.—In this point of view we may account for the oftentatious display of anxiety in Administration, for the eagernefs with which a Tellograph was apparently defired at one period, and coolly rejected at another. The Yeomanry were *to be raifed* in the firft inftance, and after the Yeomanry were raifed, and the manœuvre had anfwered its purpofe, no farther ceremony was necef- fary towards an individual.—A complimentary letter was thought a fufficient "*amende honorable*," on the part of Minifters.

The enlightened author of the pamphlet " On the Defence of Ireland," which I have before mentioned, ftrongly recommends the plan of raifing corps of Yeomanry; and high praife is unqueftion- ably due to the authors of the meafure, provided no infidious defign lurks beneath fair pretences.— If it were of no other ufe, it will pledge gentle- men to remain in the country and defend it: it is a meafure fuited to the genius of the nation; from the peafant to the peer there is a ftrong portion of mi- litary fpirit, mantling in the veins of Irifhmen.— This fpirit has been put in motion, and if it be di- rected with proper fkill and caution, it may be the

---

* Befides the private expence of the officers, the whole eftab- blifhment muft be paid for by Parliament, *independently* of the Army and Militia.

falvation

falvation of the country: but then it muft not be relied upon for fervices to which it is inadequate: the different corps of Yeomanry in the capital, the fineft body of men perhaps that exifts in Ireland, are in their formation and their fpirit the fame to all in-tents and purpofes, as the Volunteers of truly glo-rious memory; their local and profeffional fituations muft however be confidered, when we look up to them for protection againft a foreign enemy.—To protect property and their unarmed fellow-citizens, from perfonal violence and rapine, they are *more* than competent; but it would be a moft abfurd attempt to oppofe them to an invading enemy. If the merchants fhut up their counting houfes, tradef-men their fhops, if men of every occupation rufh from the city to the camp, if the defk and bar are forfaken for the fword, if the aftonifhed client ex-claims,

" Balked are the courts, and conteft is no more,"

can we fuppofe, that fuch enthufiafm would be ufe-ful or could be durable? or can we imagine that property would be more fecure in a populous city, where none were left to protect it?—In the country to collect the Yeomanry into armies, or to invite them by the powerful fpirit of emulation to the coafts, would be ftill more fatal—greater danger would be incurred, than if property never had been regularly armed. Moft certainly the proper em-ployment of fuch a force is in the protection of whatever might tempt the hand of rapine.—With

fuch

fuch internal fecurity as Yeomanry can enfure, with the trained Militia, and a *difciplined* army, Ireland might mock invafion.

Whether any attempt filently to convert the militia into fencibles *dare* be made in Ireland, I will not venture to foretel; that it has been thought of, I will not hefitate to affert. Were this fatal defign to be purfued, were the nation to believe, that our Yeomanry is the fame as that glorious army of Volunteers which, under your command, my Lord, withered the hopes of France, the country would be undone:—for in the hour of danger, a Britifh Minifter dares not leave a regiment in Ireland, which might be looked for in Great Britain.— The troops of the line in England will be largely drafted for the Weft Indies, which are obvioufly, in the eyes of the Minifter, the moft valuable appendages of the Britifh empire.—Were Ireland, in confequence of thefe meafures, to be abandoned to the protection of Fencibles and Yeomanry, no human fagacity could forefee the confequences.

I hope that my opinion with refpect to the Yeomanry * has been diftinctly expreffed. I approve highly of the inftitution, and of the motives, which animate the gentlemen who compofe it; but I de-

* I muft differ with the author of the pamphlet to which I have alluded, in one particular. He thinks the clothing of Yeomanry, of no confequence.—On the contrary, I believe, to allure the people, military uniform is effential.

precate

precate an improper ufe of them.—I dread left it
fhould become a national boaft, that we can defend
ourfelves, and left that boaft fhould be believed in
England, and fhould be too juftly appreciated in
France.

No mode of defence, however, can poffibly be
adopted, which might not derive effential advantages, from a fyftem of fpeedy and univerfal intelligence: whether we confider the internal police of
the country, or precaution againft an invading enemy, fuch a fyftem muft be of confiderable importance.—The actual eftablifhment of Telegraphs in
two powerful nations in time of war, fufficiently
protects the principle from being ftigmatized as vi-
fionary. That it would be immediately ufeful in this
kingdom muft be apparent from analogy, and from
obfervation; the opinion of fome of the beft informed men in Ireland, is decidedly in favour of a
Tellographic eftablifhment * in this country —The

* I fhall quote only the authority of the Speaker—can I
quote a better ?

The following is an extract from a letter which I received fr m
him, a few days after Lord Carhampton wrote to me, to fay that
the Lord Lieutenant wifhed to fpeak to me, on the fubject of
the Tellograph.

" I am happy that Lord Carhampton has prevailed on the
" Lord Lieutenant to fend for you—for I am perfuaded Tele-
" graphic communication is effentially neceffary, and fo far
" as I underftand other Telegraphs, I am convinced yours is
" the moft effectual."

great

great expence, which the Englifh Miniftry have without hefitation beftowed upon the Admiralty Telegraph, demonftrates clearly the value they fet upon fuch a mode of communication in England.—Are we to fuppofe that a Britifh Minifter thinks that too dear for Ireland which can be obtained at lefs than half price ?—Or is any national eftablifhment for the defence of this country, which cofts a fhilling, to be deemed extravagant by a foreign financier ?—Are the fupplies liberally granted by our Parliament to be purpofely *fenced round* with limiting claufes, to appropriate the money raifed upon the people to the uttermoft penny, left any fum fhould remain which might be difpofed of, for the advantage of the na-tion at large * ?—This is treating us in the ufual ftyle which England has affumed towards her colonial de-pendencies.

In what light Ireland is fometimes confidered by Englifhmen, we may learn from the following paffage in one of Gibbon's letters to Lord Sheffield †.— " Of Ireland, I know nothing—and while I am writ-

---

* The fums of money permitted to be laid out, or, as I have heard fome financiers exprefs it, *funk* in canals and public build-ings, are an exception in point of fact : but they are no excep-tion as to the wifhes of the Government.—So many members of Parliament are interefted in canals, that a Chancellor of the Ex-chequer, let him grumble as he might, could not refift —In this the will of the people has been effective.— Whether Ireland has been benefitted by this act of its own, requires no anfwer.

† Gibbon's Life.

" ing

" ing the decline of a great empire, I have not lei-
" fure to attend to the affairs of a remote and petty
" Province."—We fometimes accidentally perceive
objects by reflection in a glafs, which are carefully
concealed from our direct view.—From the little
attention which the Englfh Miniftry pay to the defence and protection of this kingdom, we may difcover how infignificant Ireland appears in the efti-
mation of the Britifh Cabinet. Yet it feems extraordinary, that their unfortunate experience in one
quarter of the globe fhould have made fo little impreffion upon the memory, or upon the good fenfe
of the Englifh nation.—After the lofs of " *the bright-
eft Jewel in the Britifh Crown* *,*" the remaining
gems fhould be guarded with fome increafe of care
and folicitude.

Ireland is no petty province, for fhe has an independent legiflature.—I mean not to enter into the
Sphynx's riddle of her dependent and independent
crown   I judge of her importance from her natural
and acquired refources —from her pofition in Europe
—her peculiar fufficiency to her own fubfiftence—
her obvious increafe in induftry and knowledge—
and above all by her fudden tranfition from apathy
to exertion.—Old prejudices in nations, as well as
in individuals, remain in the mind, and influence the
conduct, long after the circumftances in which they
originated are changed.   A century ago Ireland

* Lord Chatham's Speeches.

was

was a burthen to England, now fhe is her moft ufeful ally. But whatever may be the relative importance of Ireland in the eyes of a Britifh Minifter, it
cannot be imagined, that he fhould in time of danger
leave us utterly defencelefs; and though his fenfibility
may not be very acute, it muft be roufed by our
fituation.—At a moment when there was general
apprehenfion of an invafion, it was fcarcely to be
expected, that his economy fhould, in oppofition to
all other motives, have decided him to reject an eftablifhment of acknowledged and effential utility in
the defence of the kingdom.

Your Lordfhip will not, I hope, imagine, that
after the experience I have had, I am yet weak
enough to fuppofe, that any thing I can urge in
favour of the utility or policy of this eftablifhment,
will make any impreffion upon Minifterial minds.—
I addrefs myfelf to the public—to thofe in Ireland,
who have fomething to protect, Thefe things pafs
like a dream from the memory of men high in office.
They are taught to believe, that their approbation is
the meafure of all excellence, and that their opinion
neceffarily guides the judgment of all who are their
inferiors in rank.

The language of adulation deceives the ear, and
the habits of elevated ftation deceive the eye of
the great; every thing is meafured by its relation to
fome immediate object which occupies their con-
tracted fphere of vifion. That very elevation which
fhould

fhould give them a commanding view of things,
attracts a mift about them, which diftorts, and dif-
proportions diftant objects.   There is alfo fomething
in power, which operates ftrangely upon the human
heart and underftanding, which produces in thofe
who poffefs it an overweening felfifhnefs, and a
callous indifference to the interefts and feelings of
others.   They confider the lives, and talents, and
time of mankind, as at their abfolute difpofal.

" Un canonier de plus ou de moins qu'importe
t'il pourvû que le grand Seignior foit bien fervi!"
exclaimed a Turkifh minifter to the Baron de Tott—
This fhocks us from a Grand Vizier, but when there
is queftion of fending thoufands to *encounter a plague,*
the fame fentiment from a Britifh Minifter does not
aftonifh us.

It is in vain to attempt to change feelings which
are the combined refult of fituation and habit.—
Our language muft be adapted to the comprehen-
fion and difpofitions of thofe whom we addrefs.—
Talk not then to men in office of the virtue, the
wifdom, the public utility, of fuch and fuch conduct, but talk to them of its connexion with their
private policy.—This is a language which they perfectly underftand. — Calculate the probability of
their perfonal difgrace or danger, and you catch
their ear as by the fudden influence of a charm.—
They liften with the fuperftitious eagernefs of men
in love with Fortune, who know her ficklenefs,
                                                                and

and who feel how much they depend upon her
fmiles.

It requires but little fkill in prophecy, to forefee
that in thefe times of danger, when the minds of
numbers are awake to the conduct of government,
no Minifter will long maintain his power, who trufts
to the left-handed wifdom of duplicity, who is pro-
digal in all that concerns the interefts of his own
party, and economic, not to fay avaricious, in all
that concerns the happinefs of a people, and the
fafety of a kingdom.——The character of the Minifter, contrafted with that of his diftinguifhed political rival in a period original and unprecedented,
makes the danger of this little paltry and futile policy, the more evident and palpable — that fuch
conduct may not be too fatally extended to the
rejection of other projects for the defence and fafety
of the kingdom, it may not be without its ufe im-
partially to delineate the characters of thofe who
guide the empire.

Two rival Statefmen divide the opinion of the
public—oppofite in temperament, education, fyftem, and in whatever conftitutes character.—Shaded
by the prophetic mantle of his father, there was
in the firft appearance of the one fomething of fub-
limity; fplendid abilities, unufual fanctity of manners,
befpoke and juftified the confidence of his country;
—Raifed at once to a high ftation, preffed by bufinefs that muft be inftantly performed, he was obliged

liged to accept of affiftance from men hackneyed
in the ways of office, and by degrees was compelled
to relinquifh the favourite honorable refolutions of his
youth.—He did not confort with men who marked
his firft deviations.—Courtiers are not always furnifhed with a moral plumb rule to adjuft the rectitude of a
friend, though they fometimes apply it rather awk-
wardly to detect the obliquity of an enemy.—The
unbounded confidence of the public tempted the
frailty of his nature, and he fcrupled not to impofe
a little upon *the people*, who had impofed fo much
upon themfelves.

The other Statefman had a character to make.
—With the exuberant animation which ufually ac-
companies genius, he ran the eccentric round of
diffipation.—But this to him was a fhort and falutary
experiment; the fame focial nature at his firft en-
trance upon his political career led him to tolerate,
perhaps to imitate his companions: but his tafte
and judgment foon difdained the mean arts and for-
did objects of inferior ambition.—His moral character has been gradually formed by the conviction
of his underftanding, and perhaps not a fingle year
has been added to his life, which has not added to
his virtue.

The philofophic eye will perceive the influence
of character not only in the conduct of affairs, but
in the deliberation of the fenate.—When the melo-
dious voice of the Minifter fteals upon the ear,
when

when he leads us " through many a bout of lengthened fweetnefs," far away from the object which we fought, we feel as if our underftandings had been convinced, when our fenfes only have been gratified.—When he affumes the tone of argument, we admire the lucid order, the beautiful connexion, the high polifh of his oration. It is true the parts are put together with dexterity; the joinings and defects in the materials are exquifitely concealed by workmanfhip. The varnifh is fo delicate, that no rude hand ventures to deface it.—But when it yields to time, and reveals the wretched materials which it covered, we are amazed to fee fo much fkill and ingenuity beftowed upon fuch a worthlefs fabric.

His opponent rifes—We forget the orator, and fympathize with every feeling of the man.—With the energy of a mafter-hand, he ftrikes out at every blow a diftinct idea.—He never fpins the flight goffamer of fophiftry, to catch the feeble and fluttering attention; but with Herculean nerve, we fee him forge out link by link the chain of demonftration.—There is no paufe, no refpite, till the maffive length is complete and rivetted round the mind.

In a commercial nation, it is natural to look more to the financier than to the Statefman; but thefe are not times when fifcal abilities can fave an empire. Minifters who have furnifhed their memories with ftatiftical tables, and all the detail of diplomatic learning, are well qualified in times of tranquillity to trim

the

the balance of Europe, and to calculate its nice libration: but in the hour of tempeft and danger we abandon thefe refined fpeculations: we look for a Statefman, who when he finds himfelf hurried on by the irrefiftible current of affairs, governs himfelf by a bolder prudence, and who whilft the ftorm rages, dares to rely on the rapid fuggeftions of a vigorous and comprehenfive mind.

I have been infenfibly led beyond my original intention, and have touched upon what I hope to make the fubject of a future letter.—The extent of your Lordfhip's indulgence, though I have tried it, I fcarcely know, but I hope you will pardon me for endeavouring to mix fomething of higher import, with what might appear only a perfonal concern.— The fame apology will I hope be accepted by the public, who will pardon me for having intruded myfelf fo long upon their attention.—I confider the tranfaction I have laid before them, rather as a public than a private concern.—Had I merely experienced a vulgar difappointment in ambition, had I fimply difcovered duplicity in a court, I fhould not think the novelty of my difcovery, or the bitternefs of my difappointment, would much intereft the public. But furely the public has fome intereft in knowing, what offers are made to government for the defence of the country, how thofe offers are received, and what treatment an individual meets with, who, without the common motives of emolument or ambition, applies himfelf with fome perfeverance, and,

as

as it is allowed even by thofe who reject his fervices, with fome fuccefs, to perfect an object of national utility. The few who ftudy politics as a
fcience, who confider events not fo much as to their
abfolute as their relative magnitude, who mark the
fpirit of the times, the temper of thofe who govern,
and of thofe who fubmit, will from flight omens
draw important auguries.—" Take a ftraw," fays
Selden, " and throw it up into the air, you may fee
" by that, which way the wind is, which you fhall
" not do by cafting up a ftone."

Even thofe, who do not call themfelves politicians,
may find fome advantage in looking into public
meafures. The habit of confidering, and judging
of affairs improves the fagacity of *the people*.—The
letters of Secretaries and Commanders in Chief
can be contemplated at leifure and without awe in a
printed form, and perfons who are apt to feel their
underftandings bewildered by the myfteries of office, when the veil is fairly drawn, will be glad to
difcover that plain common fenfe is competent to
difcufs and decide *.—Whilft every thing can be
fully laid before the public, there is no danger that
the people fhould be oppreffed; and thofe who
attack the liberties of mankind, have more to dread
from the invifible union of enlightened minds, than

* I appeal to every man's recollection of his feelings upon
the publication of Mr. Boyd's negociation with Mr. Pitt, and of
Lord Fitzwilliam's and Admiral Cornwallis's with other members of adminiftration.

from

from all the cabals of faction, or all the leagues of ignorant force.

Cardinal Mazarine, when he heard any comments upon his meafures, ufed to exclaim—" Let them "*fay* what they pleafe, provided they let me *do* what " I pleafe."—The people have more reafon to be content with their fhare in this divifion of power, than the fhort-fighted politician apprehended. The defpotic Cardinal's maxim, with a trifling alteration, may be juftly adopted as an axiom by a free nation.

" Let us fay and write, whatever conftitutional liberty allows, and let Minifters attempt what they dare."

I have the honor to be,

my Lord,

with the greateft refpect,

your Lordfhip's

obliged and humble fervant,

RICHARD LOVELL EDGEWORTH.

Edgeworthftown,
December 13th, 1796.

POST-

POSTSCRIPT.

ON Friday the 30th of December, at night, I received authentic intelligence that the enemy were on our coasts.—I immediately sent a servant express to Mr. Pelham with a letter offering to erect the Tellographs, which I have in Dublin, on any line that government should direct, and to bring *my own men along with* me; or to join the army with my portable Tellographs to reconnoitre and convey intelligence.

My servant was sent back with a note from Mr. Pelham, containing his compliments, and the promise of a speedy answer.—No answer has ever reached me.

Upon such an emergency I could, with the improvements which I have mentioned in my letter of the 19th of September, and with the assistance of my friends, have established a communication be-

D

tween

tween Dublin and any of our ports before the
French fleet had left the coaft; and had my offer
been accepted, it fhould not have coft government
a fhilling.

I did not feel mortified at this neglect, becaufe
I was fenfible, that the difpleafure of the public
would not light upon me; but I felt, and feel
much concern in being deprived of an opportunity
of alleviatiñg the anxiety and diftrefs of thoufands,
and of faving an enormous expence to this country;
I have been informed from various quarters that a
Tellograph has been moft earneftly wifhed for;
danger quickens the perceptions of individuals to
national interefts, and every practicable fcheme of
defence is confidered with an eagernefs very different from the apathy of general fafety.—Government had not the fame feelings as individuals, or it
would have taken means to inform the people with
certainty and expedition: nor is it to be expected,
that in a fyftem fupported by patronage any fortu-
nate opportunity for profufion fhould be fuffered to
efcape—whether the anxiety of the Caftle was pro-
portioned to the real difficulty or danger, I am at a
lofs to conjecture; of this however I am certain,
that the confufed, and contradictory reports pub-
lifhed under the fanction of Government, and which
have appeared at fecond-hand in the Englifh pa-
pers, cannot upon a reperufal convey any agreeable fenfations either to themfelves or to the peo-

8   ple:

ple: the fame narrownefs of defign is obvious in every thing, the fame confidence in fortune, and the fame indifference about the future.—The critic was not much miftaken, who afferted, that the moft interefting circumftance in the tragedy of Iphigenia in Euripides is the direction of the winds. Which of the heathen Deities we have propitiated in our favour I cannot tell; it certainly was not Mercury !

I fhall not expatiate upon the advantages that might have been obtained, and the evils which might have been avoided, by another fyftem; becaufe the feelings of individuals, and the good fenfe of the public, will fuggeft more than I could enumerate or imagine. I fhall only fubmit a few queries to the confideration of Government, and to the judgment of the country.

How many hours elapfed from the firft appearance of the enemy on the coaft to the time that it was known by Government * ?

How many minutes would have intervened had a Tellograph been previoufly eftablifhed ?

---

* An accurate journal of the weather is kept at my houfe, one column of which has for feveral months been appropriated to regifter the comparative clearnefs of the atmofphere ; and but one period of 24 hours has been too hazy for *my* Tellograph fince the 26th of December.

How

How many days were wasted in fruitless wishes for an English fleet?

In how many hours could a message have been sent from Cork by Donaghadee to London, had the proposed plan of communication been adopted?

Would it have been entirely agreeable to the English ministry to have received immediate intelligence from Ireland upon a late occasion?

Would it have been necessary with a Tellograph to have given such contradictory orders to the troops, to have harassed them with forced marches, and to have discouraged them with countermarches? or did not these orders plainly proceed from the want of intelligence and from indecision?

Would the general alarm have produced the same anxiety amongst individuals if intelligence had been conveyed from hour to hour with expedition?

Would the same pecuniary embarrassments, the same distress, the same stagnation of trade, the same bankruptcies have been the consequence of an attempted invasion, if immediate communication could have been kept up between distant correspondents, and had the real situation of affairs been constantly and regularly laid before the public?

What

What will be the additional expence charged to the public for the movements occafioned by hurry and uncertainty ?

Will not every negle&, and every falfe ftatement be known in a few days by the enemy, as well as by our friends ?

Might not the Englifh Minifter have been fpared the ridicule of haranguing upon the improbability of an attack upon Ireland at the very time that the enemy was upon its coaft ?

Was it a ftroke of humour in Mr. Pitt, or a glimpfe of his father's prophetic fpirit, to fay (December 30th), " I fhould not be furprifed if in " their rage for annexing territory which does not " belong to them, they (the French) fhould make " Ireland part of France, one, and indivifible ?"

May not the favourite policy of divide and conquer, eventually be reverfed, and become divide and *be conquered ?*

May not the Greek proverb, "half is better than the whole," be mifapplied in governing a country ?

Should not the errors of the paft be leffons for the future ? Or, after all, will it be thought, that as

the

the enemy have been once upon our coaft, *for that very reafon* they can never come again.

Muft we not admire the piety of our Chief Go-
vernor, who, in his meffage to Parliament,

" Like the good bifhop with a meeker air,
" Admits, and leaves us *Providence's* care !"

THE END.